XXX

I Love you from
zuzia
Mrs.

First published by Parragon in 2011

Parragon
Queen Street House
4 Queen Street
Bath BA1 1HE, UK

ISBN 978-1-4454-3294-6

Printed in China

My Complete Disney Princess Book

Cinderella and the Lost Mice

By E.C. Llopis
Illustrated by: IBOIX and Michael Inman

The stars twinkled in the clear night sky as the Prince twirled Cinderella outside to dance.

"Are you cold, my dear?" the Prince asked his princess.

"Just a bit, but –"

Smiling, the Prince reached for a box he had hidden under a bench. Inside was a beautiful winter coat.

"Oh, it's simply lovely!" Cinderella exclaimed. "Thank you!"

The next morning Cinderella showed her coat to Suzy the mouse. "Isn't the Prince kind to me?" she said.

"Nice-a! Nice-a!" Suzy nodded and nuzzled the warm coat.

Cinderella didn't notice that Suzy had just come in from the cold. The tiny mouse was shivering even though the room was warm!

Just then, Gus and Jaq scampered up onto
Cinderella's dressing table.
"Cinderelly! Cinderelly!" they chattered.
Cinderella didn't hear them as she rushed off to meet
the Prince. She didn't know that they were cold, too!

Soon several more cold and shivering mice entered the room. They sat in front of the fire until their teeth stopped chattering. The poor mice had spent the night in the freezing attic! They hoped Cinderella would let them stay in her warm room. But there was a problem.

"Shoo, shoo!" The cruel housekeeper barged into the room and began chasing the mice! "You're making the whole castle dirty!" she shouted. "I should have the gardener haul you away!"

She was the reason that the mice were cold – and scared. They stayed in the attic to hide from her!

The mice scrambled back to the chilly attic, not knowing where else to go.

"Cinderelly," Gus sighed. They needed her help!

Suddenly – *WHAM!!* – the gardener slammed cages over the mice and scooped them up!

"Now take them outside!" shrieked the housekeeper. "Take them far enough away that they never return!"

Of course, Cinderella had no idea what had happened as she and the Prince strolled along the castle grounds.

"Let's go to the stables!" Cinderella said suddenly. "We can say hello to the horses."

"And maybe take a ride?" the Prince asked hopefully.

"Lovely idea!" Cinderella replied.

Soon Cinderella and the Prince were riding through the countryside near the castle. They saw the gardener doing something in one of the fields.

"Hello!" shouted the Prince. "It's too cold to be working outside!"

But the gardener didn't seem to hear the Prince.

When the Prince and princess returned to the stables, the Prince asked, "Do you think the gardener was acting oddly?"

"Perhaps he was distracted," Cinderella replied thoughtfully. "It must be hard to do much gardening when the ground is frozen."

But the gardener was not distracted about gardening. He was worried about the mice! He knew that they would freeze in the fields.

"All right." he said to his helpers. "Now don't mention this to the housekeeper, but I want to bring these poor mice to the stables."

So they took the grateful mice to their new home and even fed them.

The mice nestled together in the barn, but as night approached, they just got colder. Finally the horses allowed them to snuggle up in their manes to keep warm.

"Thassa nice-a," Gus said sleepily.

Meanwhile, Cinderella was beginning to worry. Where were her little friends?

"Jaq and Gus!" she thought suddenly. "They wanted to talk to me this morning, but I left in a rush to see the Prince. I wonder if they needed to tell me something."

Cinderella was searching the palace trying to find her friends when she ran into the Prince.

"Why, hello!" the Prince said cheerfully. "Are you looking for the same person I am?"

"Person?" asked Cinderella. "Why, no! I'm looking for the mice!"

"Ah," said the Prince. "And I am looking for the housekeeper who apparently threw them out of the castle today. She said they were dirty!"

"Dirty! Oh, no!" Cinderella cried. "They're not dirty. And besides, they'll freeze outside!"

"Don't worry, my dear. The mice have found a new friend." The Prince then told Cinderella about the gardener and what he had done.

Together, Cinderella and the Prince went to the stables, where they found and thanked the gardener. Then Cinderella awakened the mice who were snuggled comfortably in the horses' manes.

"Cinderelly! Cinderelly!" the mice shouted happily.

A few nights later, there was a grand ball – with the gardener as the guest of honour. The cruel housekeeper now peeled potatoes in the kitchen. She would not be bothering the mice again. Meanwhile, the mice celebrated with a banquet of their own. And as for the horses, they got extra apples all around!

The End

Tiana and Her Loyal Friend

By Natalie Amanda Leece
Illustrated by Studio IBOIX and Walt Sturrock

It was a balmy afternoon in New Orleans. Big Daddy was in the mood for some good food and good times with friends.

"Charlotte honey!" he called out to his daughter. "How about going to Tiana's Palace for supper tonight –"

"Oh, Daddy, that would be wonderful! Just give me a minute to change."

Later, as they drove off, nobody noticed Stella the hound asleep in the back of the car!

But Stella didn't mind. In fact, the one thing that woke her up was the smell of Tiana's beignets when they reached the restaurant. Stella loved Tiana's beignets, so the hound followed her nose right into the restaurant's back kitchen.

"Big Daddy! Charlotte!" Princess Tiana warmly welcomed her friends. "Would you like to sit with my mama?"

"Why, I can't think of anyone better to share my supper with than Eudora," Big Daddy replied.

After the last jazz number was played, Prince
Naveen's parents, the king and queen of Maldonia,
got up to leave, offering Eudora a ride home.

"Why, thank you," Eudora said. Turning to Princess Tiana, she added,
"I have never heard the band play quite so well as tonight. And that new
gumbo – absolutely delicious. I'll see you later, sweetheart."

As everyone said their goodbyes, still nobody knew about Stella....

...not until Louis entered the kitchen for his evening meal with the rest of the band.

"Grrr! Woof!" Stella was terrified of the giant alligator.

"Oh, now hold on, little dog!" Louis spoke to Stella. "I'm not here to eat you. I just wanted a taste of the chefs' new gumbo!"

The kitchen staff backed away. They just heard growls coming from the dog and the gator.

Princess Tiana and Prince Naveen also heard the commotion as they re-entered the restaurant after bidding their friends and family good night.

As soon as the prince and princess entered the kitchen, they saw a very frightened Stella plastered against a wall, barking at Louis.

"What is going on with you two?" Princess Tiana said, concerned for Stella.

"Oh, Stella," Princess Tiana said, gently petting the dog. "It's just Louis. He wouldn't hurt anybody."

"That's true!" Naveen cried as he put his arm around Louis. "Louis? He is nothing but a big guy with a bigger heart."

"Go ahead, Stella," Princess Tiana encouraged the dog. "Naveen will hold onto Louis, and you just walk right over to them."

Cautiously, Stella walked toward Louis, with Tiana by her side.

Stella sniffed Louis and then turned back towards the food. Tiana giggled. Naveen giggled. Louis wanted to giggle, but he thought he might scare Stella all over again.

It didn't take long for the staff of Tiana's Palace to put together a supper, made up of that evening's leftovers. Prince Naveen played the ukulele, and Tiana made some of her special beignets – just for Stella.

Princess Tiana had to smile. These were truly the good times her father had imagined having at their restaurant.

Before dawn, the prince and princess dropped Stella off at the LaBouff estate. No one had even noticed she was missing yet!

"Good night, Stella," Princess Tiana said, giving the dog a big hug. "And don't be a stranger. When I stop by, I expect you to come out and get your own beignets."

Stella gave one last woof and went towards the house. She had had the best night of her life.

The End

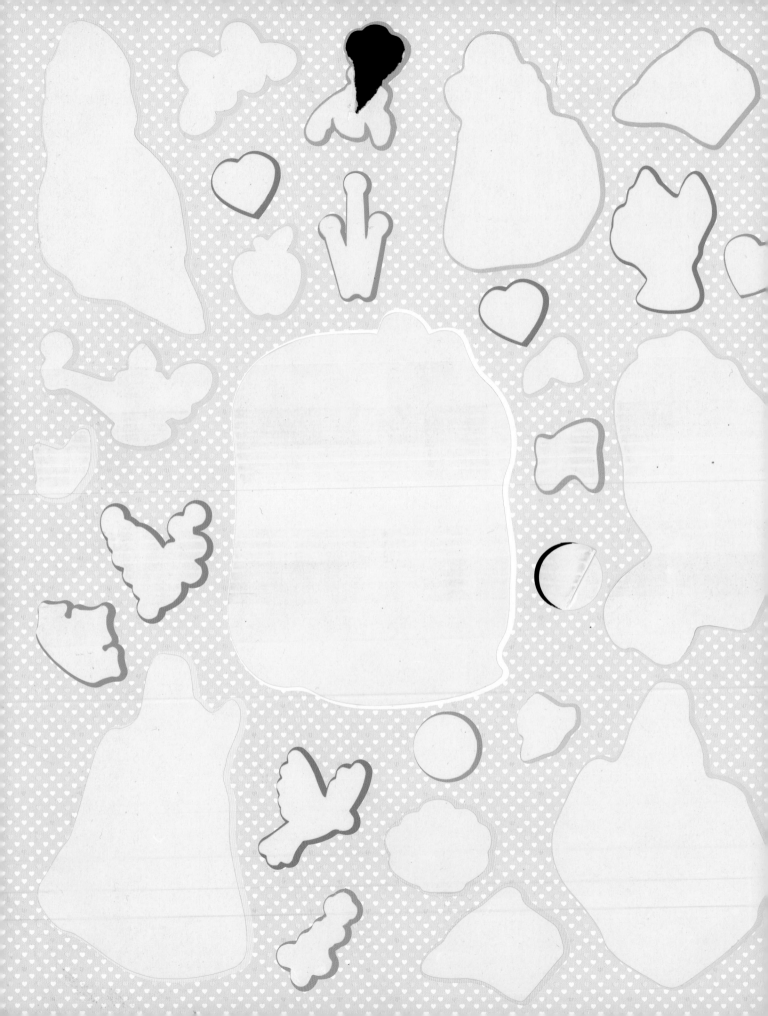

Magical Activities

Complete these princess puzzles and activities,
then turn to page 100 to find the answers.

"Magic Mirror on the wall, who is the fairest one of all?" Draw yourself in the mirror.

Doc and Dopey are making a necklace for Snow White. Can you color it?

1 = RED   2 = YELLOW   3 = BLUE

Hi ho, hi ho. Who is off to work?
Cross out all the "i"s and "t"s to find out.

1. TDIOIPTEIY _____
2. IBTASITIHTFIUL _____
3. STINEETZIY _____
4. TSLIETEPTIY _____
5. IHTAIIPTPIY _____
6. IGRTIUMTPIY _____
7. TDIITOTIICT _____

Look at this picture of Snow White and her forest friends.
Then answer the questions below.

1. How many birds? _3_

2. How many butterflies? _4_

3. How many rabbits? _5̶3_

4. How many squirrels? _2_

5. How many turtles? _1_

Help the Prince find the missing glass slipper. Circle the slipper that matches the one in the Prince's hand.

Draw a picture of yourself at the ball.

Prince Charming's Ball

Find the following words in the pumpkin carriage below.
(Hint: You will find the words going down and across.)

Cinderella ✓
prince ✓
slipper ✓
Gus ✓
midnight ✓
mice ✓
pumpkin ✓
ball ✓
stepmother ✓
gown ✓

a s t d p r s e m g
r m u d r i t s i n
t p r i n c e p d r
s p u m t r s l i s
g u s a s s p i g l
o m i c e s r p h a
w p b a l l t p t i
n k r s t m o e l e
c i n d e r e r l a
r n m p d u r p r w

Help Cinderella's friends finish the surprise! Colour the dress pink, the stars yellow and the hearts purple.

Can you match these sentences with the pictures they describe?
Write the number of each sentence in the
circle beside the correct picture.

3) Cinderella's friends help her get dressed.

2) The Fairy Godmother comforts Cinderella.

1) The shoe fits!

Help Prince Phillip save Princess Aurora.
Connect the dots to reveal his magic sword.

Help Prince Phillip find his way to the castle so he can awaken Princess Aurora with a kiss.

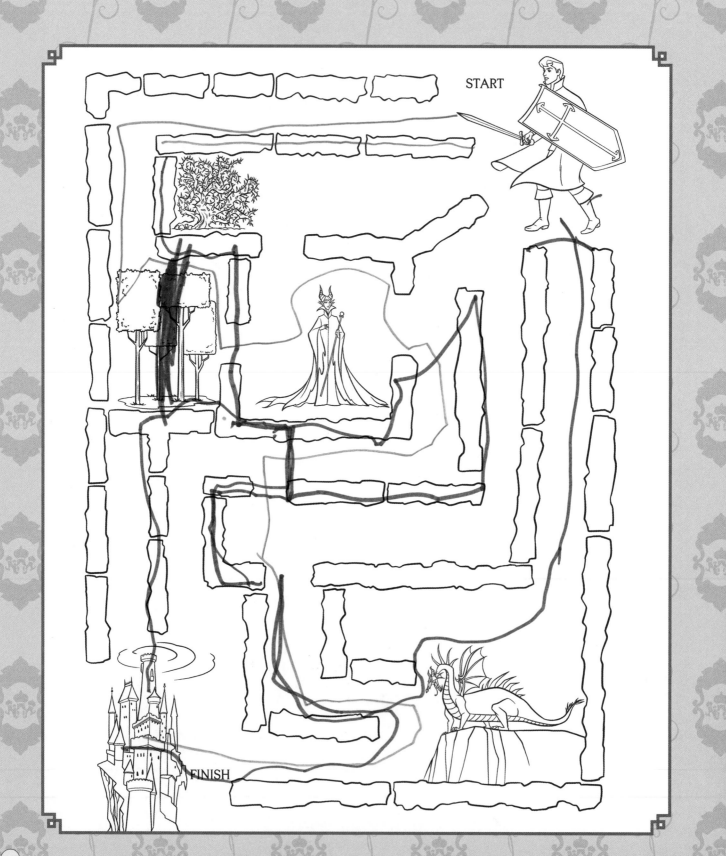

START

FINISH

What gifts do the fairies give to Princess Aurora when she is a baby?
Use the code below to find out.

A	B	C	D	E	F	G	H	I	J	K	L	M	N	O	P	Q	R	S	T	U	V	W	X	Y	Z
1	2	3	4	5	6	7	8	9	10	11	12	13	14	15	16	17	18	19	20	21	22	23	24	25	26

Flora gives the gift of _Beauty_.

2	5	1	21	20	25

Fauna gives the gift of _SONG_.

19	15	14	7

Number these pictures in the order they happened.

Connect the dots to see Briar Rose's dance partner.

There's magic happening! Can you find 6 things
that are different in the second picture?

Use crayons or pens to colour Ariel, Flounder and Sebastian.

Look at this picture of Ariel, Eric and their animal friends. Then answer the questions below.

1. How many seagulls? _2_   3. How many fish? _3_

2. How many frogs? _3_   4. How many flamingos? _3_

Join Ariel as she explores the shipwreck!
Look for the names listed on the right in the puzzle below.
(Hint: You will find them going down and across.)

Prince Eric

Ariel

Flounder

King Triton

Max

Scuttle

Sebastian

Ursula

```
k r s e a d t c g m p
i e p a z u l l r a r
n o u r s u l a r f i
g d n i u o s s y l n
t e r e p a c r w o c
r l a l d n u o d u e
i s e b a s t i a n e
t d p r e g t s e d r
o r m a x p l t n e i
n i n c s s e d w r c
```

Eric and Ariel are collecting shells, stones and sticks on the beach. They've arranged them in two different patterns.

Can you finish each pattern by filling in the blank spaces with shells, stones or branches?

1. ___ ___ ___

2. ___ ___

Everyone in the kitchen wants to cheer Belle up with a show.
Find the matching dishes, cups, forks and knives.
Circle the ones that are the same.

There are 7 odd and silly things happening in this picture. Can you find them all? Here are some hints:

- What's Gaston wearing on his head?
- There's a fire somewhere.
- Someone is walking on his hands.
- What an odd looking bicycle.

- Take a look at Gaston's feet.
- It looks like Belle is going swimming!
- An animal has escaped from the farm!

Be a reader like Belle!
Cut along the dotted lines to create two bookmarks.

Let's read a story together!

Reading can take you to far off places!

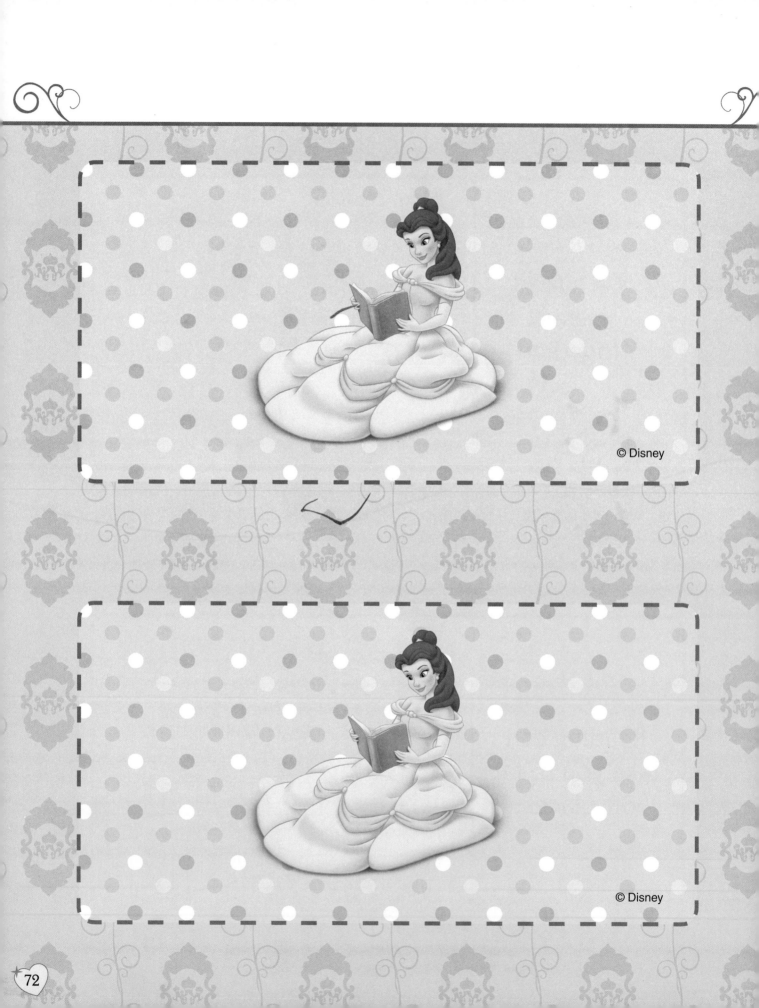

© Disney

© Disney

Help Belle and the Beast build a snowman with eyes,
arms, a nose and a mouth. Don't forget his hat and scarf!

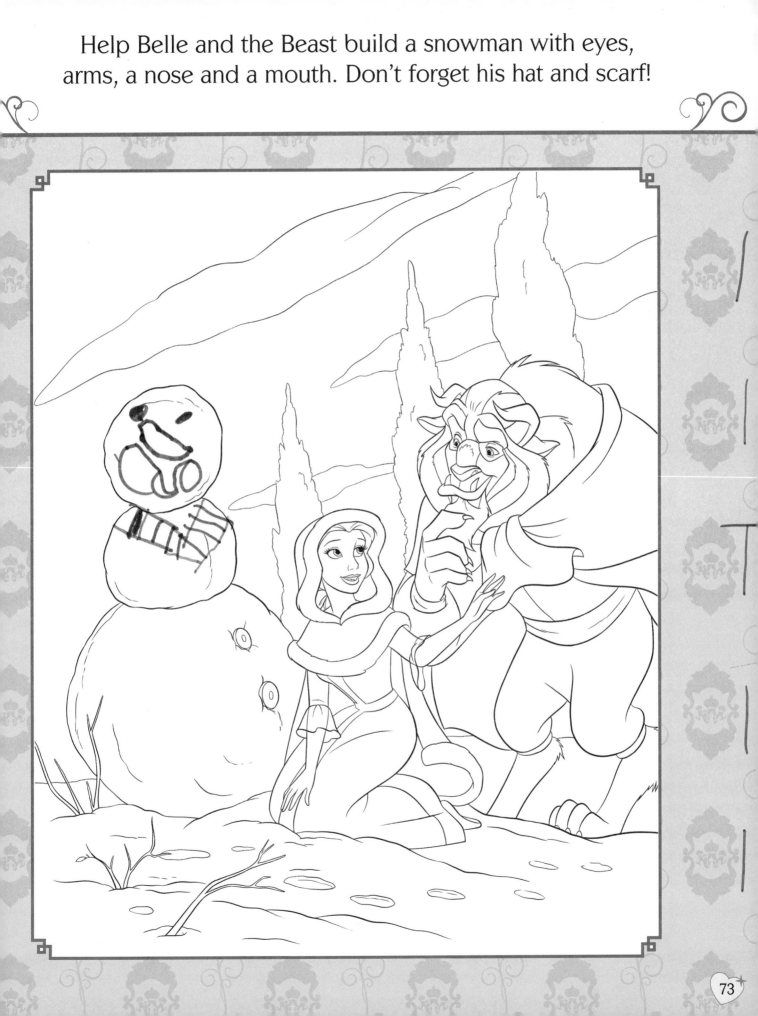

The Beast's Magic Mirror lets you see anyone you want.
Draw the person you would like to see in the Magic Mirror.

Write the names of the objects below in the crossword puzzle.

Across

1   4   6   7   8

Down

2   3   4   5

Can you find the following 10 objects hidden in the picture below?

- A glove
- A car
- A beach ball

- A rooster
- A purse
- A brush

- A cake
- A broom
- A pair of boots

- A comb

What kind of pet do Jasmine and Aladdin have?
Cross out all the "U"s and "B"s to find the answer to the riddle.

Bau ufublubuyiunbg bucuabur-bupubuetb!

Use crayons or pens to colour the palace and the city of Agrabah.

Jasmine and Aladdin are ready for a reading adventure!
Cut along the dotted lines to create two bookmarks.

Read a book and discover a whole new world!

Every book holds a new adventure!

© Disney

© Disney

Jasmine wore the same outfit and accessories twice this week.
What two days did she wear the same things?

Tuesday and _Friday_

Tuesday   Wednesday   Thursday

Monday

Friday   Saturday   Sunday

Look at this picture of Pocahontas, John Smith and their woodland friends. Then answer the questions below.

How many deer? ———   How many rabbits? ———

How many squirrels?———   How many raccoons? ———

Help Pocahontas find her way through the forest to John Smith.

FINISH

START

How many butterflies do you see?
Write the number.

I see _____ butterflies.

Meeko watches his friend Pocahontas from four different spots. Can you find all the Meekos?

Complete this scene with the small pictures below.
Write the letter of each picture in the correct white box.

One of the canoes below matches Pocahontas's canoe. Can you find it?

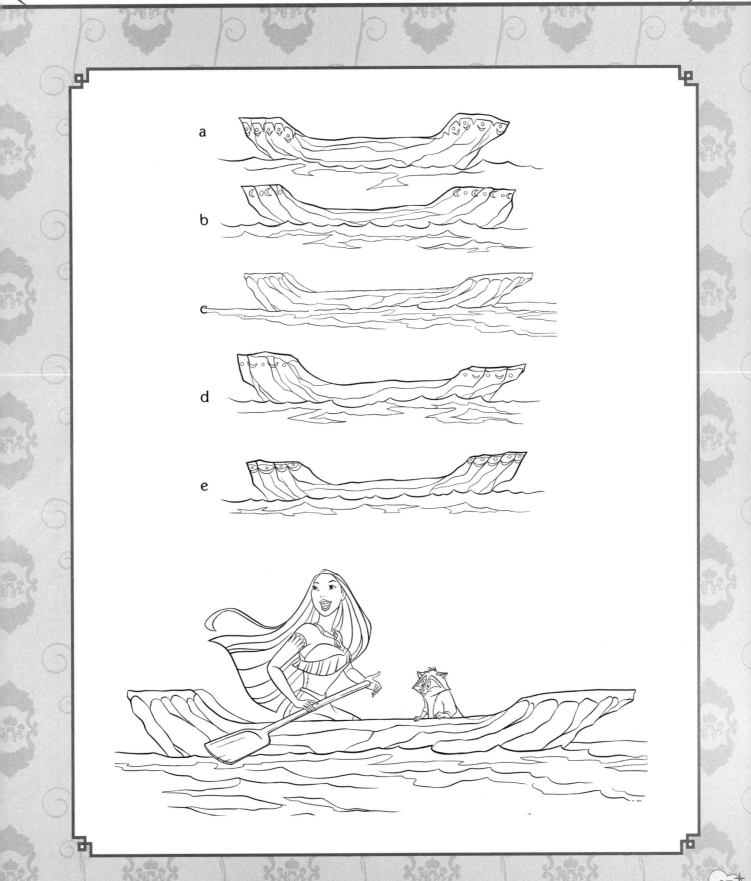

Write the names of the animals and objects below in the crossword puzzle.

Across

Down

Mulan needs to get to the Emperor. Can you help her?

START

FINISH

Help Shang train his men.
Can you find 6 things that are different in the second picture?

Complete this scene with the small pictures below.
Write the letter of each picture in the correct white box.

Help the Matchmaker find the two Mulans who are the same.

1

2

3

4

5

6

7

8

9

Write the names of the people and things below in the crossword puzzle.

Across

3

5

7

Down

1

2

4

6

Each of the rows below must have FOUR princesses: Snow White, Aurora, Cinderella and Belle.
Fill each empty box with the correct letter.

Have an adult help you cut out each picture, punch a hole at the top, and thread a ribbon through the hole. Then decorate your room with these beautiful princesses!

Draw a picture of yourself as a princess on the back of the decorations.

© Disney

© Disney

© Disney

© Disney

Ask an adult to help you cut out each picture, punch a hole at the top and thread a ribbon through the hole. Then decorate your room with these beautiful princesses!

Draw a picture of yourself as a princess on the back of the decorations.

© Disney

© Disney

© Disney

© Disney

Draw a line from each princess to her shadow.

Answers

Page 52
1. Dopey, 2. Bashful,
3. Sneezy, 4. Sleepy,
5. Happy, 6. Grumpy,
7. Doc

Page 53
1. 3 Birds, 2. 4 Butterflies,
3. 3 rabbits, 4. 2 Squirrels,
5. 1 turtle.

Page 54

Page 56

Page 58
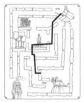

Page 60

Page 61
Flora gives the gift of BEAUTY
Fauna gives the gift of SONG

Page 62

Page 64

Page 66
1. 2 Seagulls, 2. 3 Frogs,
3. 3 Fish, 4. 3 Flamingos

Page 67

Page 68

Page 69

Page 70

Page 75

Page 76

Page 77
A Flying Carpet.

Page 81
Tuesday and thursday.

Page 82
3 deer, 4 squirrels, 2 rabbits
and 1 raccoon.

Page 83

Page 84
I see 22 butterflies

Page 85

Page 86

Page 87
C matches Pocahonta's Canoe.

Page 88

Page 89

Page 90
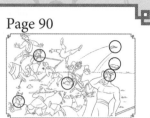

Page 91

Page 92
7 and 9

Page 93

Page 94

D			
			A
			C
B			

Page 99

Beautiful Colouring

Use your favourite colouring pens or crayons to
make these princess pictures look magical.

The Dwarfs learn many things from Snow White.

"Do you need help, little turtle?"

The Dwarfs are cleaning the house to surprise Snow White.

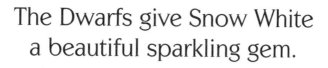

The Dwarfs give Snow White a beautiful sparkling gem.

Music is the language of the heart!

Snow White and the Prince take a walk in the meadow under the moonlight.

There are so many apples ready for picking!

A little bird tells Snow White he is hungry for seeds.

The squirrels find a red ribbon for Snow White's hair.

Snow White calls the Dwarfs for dinner.

The Prince has a beautiful horse
for Snow White to ride!

Cinderella starts the day with a happy song.

Cinderella has made a special treat for Jaq's birthday.

The mice give Lucifer a new look.

Prince Charming and Cinderella
take Bruno for a brisk walk.

With help from her animal friends, Cinderella
sews a new suit for Prince Charming.

Cinderella's favourite vegetables
are broccoli and tomatoes.

"Hmmm, where is my other shoe?"

Cinderella gives her horse a treat.

Cinderella has decided what kind of pie to make.

Prince Charming and Cinderella enjoy
an anniversary dance.

The ducks look forward to Cinderella's visits.

Do you think Aurora likes blue or pink?

Aurora arrives home after a walk in the woods.

Aurora adds small candy roses to a birthday cake.

The squirrels like playing among the yellow flowers.

Using her imagination, Aurora tells a story.

Everyone in the kingdom celebrates Aurora's birthday.

Let's get ready for a picnic!

Prince Phillip and Aurora go for
a ride through the country.

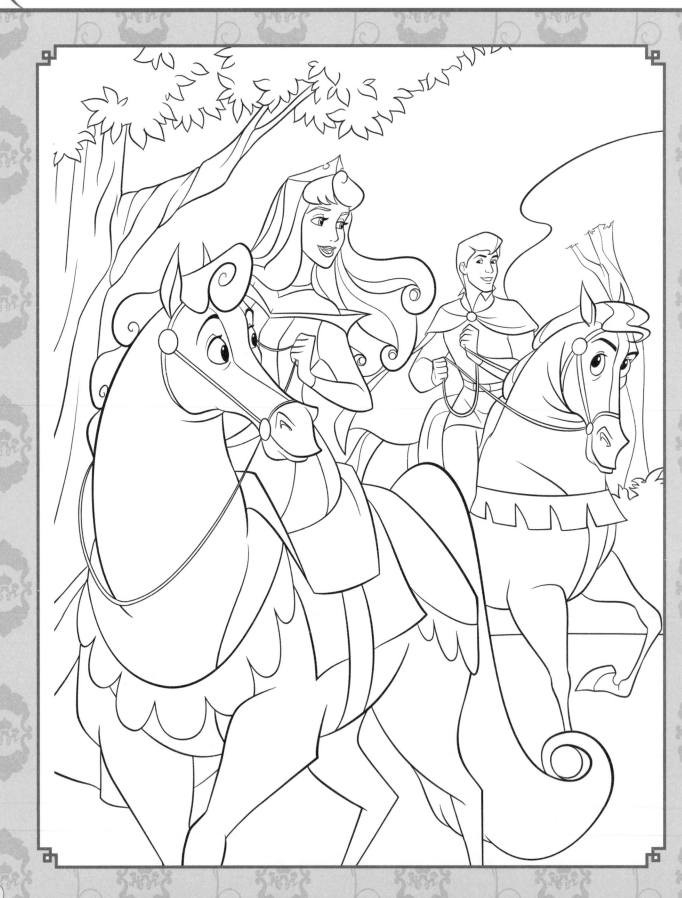

Aurora needs help deciding which tiara to wear today.

Aurora loves listening to music.

This momma bird has just had babies.

"I love you with all my heart!"

Ariel loves being a princess in a castle.

Scuttle makes up funny stories about objects.

Sebastian helps Ariel build a sand castle.

Flounder cares very much for his friend Ariel.

Ariel's friends are always playing around.

Ariel offers Scuttle something from the human world.

Ariel's family will always love her.

Ariel will never forget her life under the sea.

Sebastian likes to help out whenever he can.

"My love for you is as big as the ocean!"

Ariel and her underwater pals enjoy a friendly race.

Belle reads to the children of the village.

Belle loves her father very much.

Gaston is sure he will marry a pretty girl like Belle.

Chip sings a song for his mother, Mrs Potts.

The Prince and Belle read their favourite book together.

Belle remembers when the Prince
was not so handsome.

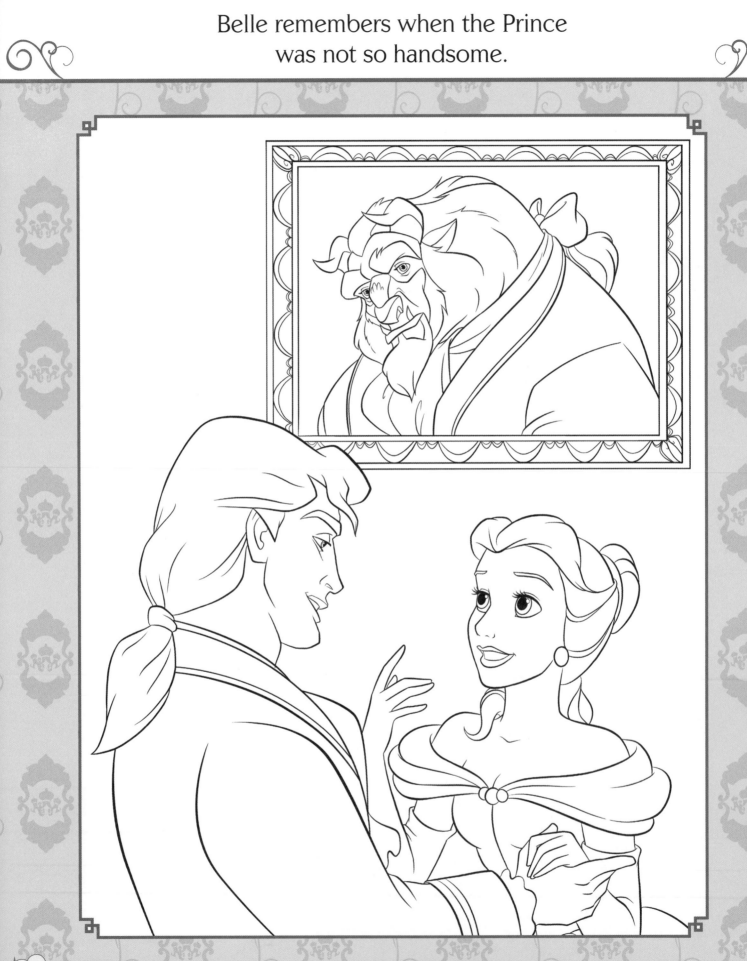

There are lots of things to buy today.

Belle keeps a diary of her happy memories.

"What do you think we could get
Chip for his birthday?"

Belle and the Prince have dinner together every night.

The library is usually quiet, but not today!

Jasmine is lucky to have a good friend like Rajah.

Jewels are nice, but love is more precious.

Aladdin and Jasmine monkey around with Abu.

Jasmine and Aladdin try to count all the stars.

It is time to do the shopping.

"Don't be afraid, it is only a mouse!"

Aladdin gives Jasmine a beautiful new dress.

The Genie always makes Jasmine's day.

Tonight is perfect for a ride in
the magic of the moonlight.

Jasmine gives her shoes to someone who lost hers.

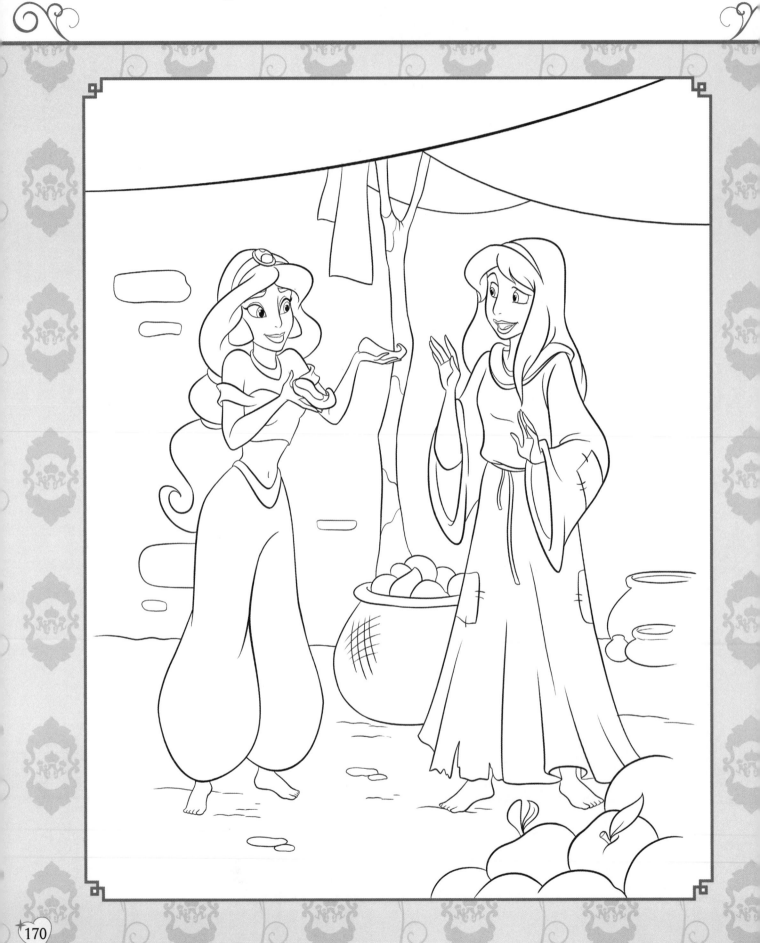

Being in love shows Jasmine a whole new world.

Tiana wishes upon a star.

Tiana looks beautiful in the bayou!

Naveen and Tiana make a perfect couple.

Aurora and the
Helpful Dragon

By Barbara Bazaldua
Illustrated by Studio IBOIX and Gabriella Matta

"I'll race you to the lookout point!" Princess Aurora called to Prince Phillip as they galloped through the forest one sunny autumn morning. She sped away on her horse, Moonlight, with Prince Phillip close behind.

Just as Aurora and Phillip rounded a bend, they heard a funny noise. A small dragon popped out from behind a tree and scampered towards Aurora.

"Oh, he's so cute!" Aurora exclaimed as she dismounted.
"Grrgrrgrr?" the little dragon murmured, clambering into Aurora's lap.
But Phillip wanted to protect his wife. "Dragons can be dangerous!"
The little dragon shook his head, no.

"I think he's saying he's not dangerous," Aurora laughed. "Please, let's take him home. I'm going to name him Crackle!"

"He does seem like a harmless little fellow," Phillip agreed.

But Moonlight was still afraid. She tossed her mane and pawed the ground. Crackle's tail drooped sadly. Then he grinned his funny little grin. Suddenly, he licked Moonlight's nose with his long, warm tongue. Moonlight blinked with surprise and nuzzled Crackle under the chin. The little dragon giggled.

"Moonlight likes Crackle!" Aurora laughed.

When Phillip and Aurora rode into the courtyard, the three fairies were hanging banners for King Stefan and the Queen who were coming for a ball that night.

"Come, my dear, let's practise dancing!" Phillip said to his princess.

But Flora gasped when she saw Crackle. "Dragons can be dangerous."

"Remember the last one!" Fauna added.

"Oooh, I think he's sweet," Merryweather spoke up.

"Grrrgrr," Crackle babbled.

"He thinks you're sweet, too," Aurora told Merryweather as Prince Phillip swept his princess across the courtyard.

Just then, Crackle noticed a kitten in Fauna's workbasket.

Crackle listened to the cute kitten purring. Crackle scrunched up his mouth and closed his eyes.

"Purrgrr, purrgrr!" Crackle tried to purr. Clouds of smoke puffed from his nose and mouth.

"Aachoo! Aachooooie! Ah-ah-ah-CHOO!" The fairies sneezed so hard that they fluttered backwards.

"Please – achoo – stop trying to purr!" Fauna exclaimed.

Crackle looked sad for a moment. Then he saw the kitten playing with a ball of yarn from the workbasket, and his eyes lit up. He snatched a ball of yarn with his mouth. Whoosh! – it caught fire. Merryweather put the fire out with her wand.

"Oh, Crackle," Aurora said gently. "You're not a kitten. You're a dragon." Crackle's lower lip trembled.

Just then, Crackle saw Phillip leading the horses into the stables. A dog followed Phillip barking and wagging its tail. Crackle wagged his tail and ran to the stables, too.

"Woofgrr, woofgrr," he tried to bark. Flames shot from his mouth and caught some straw on fire. Phillip poured water on the burning straw.

"You're not a dog," he said kindly, shooing Crackle away.

When Aurora saw Crackle creep from the stable, she carried him into the castle and cuddled him on a window seat. A bird was singing outside. Crackle's ears perked up and his eyes shone hopefully.

"LAAAlaagrr!" he bellowed.

King Hubert heard the racket and rushed into the room.

"Oh, my, my, my! How did a dragon get in here?" he blustered.

Frightened by the king, Crackle jumped from the window seat and ran into the garden. Aurora ran after him. At last she found the little dragon sitting beside a waterfall that splashed down from one pool to another. Crackle was studying a fish swimming in the lowest pool.

Before Aurora could stop him, Crackle splashed into the water. The startled fish leaped into a higher pool.

"Crackle, you're not a fish!" Aurora exclaimed as she pulled Crackle from the pool. "You're not a kitten, or a dog, or a bird either. You're a dragon!"

Tears rolled down Crackle's face. "Grrgrrgrr," he sobbed.

Suddenly, Aurora understood. "Do you think no one will like you because you're a dragon?" she asked.

Crackle nodded and whimpered sadly.

"Crackle, you can't change being a dragon," Aurora said kindly. "But you don't have to be a dangerous dragon. You can be a brave, helpful dragon."

Crackle stopped crying. "Grrgrrgrrgrr?" he growled hopefully.

Before Aurora could answer, thunder boomed. Wind blew black clouds over the sun. Aurora snatched up Crackle. She reached the castle doors just as the rain began to pour down.

Everyone was gathered in the grand hallway, watching the storm.

"I'm afraid King Stefan and the Queen might lose their way on the road above the cliffs," Prince Phillip said, his voice filled with concern. "I should ride out to help."

Aurora looked at Crackle. "Do you want to show everyone that you're a brave and helpful dragon?" she asked.

"GRRRgrrrgrr!" Crackle exclaimed enthusiastically.

"Fly to the top of the highest castle tower," Aurora explained. "Then blow the largest, brightest flames you can."

Aurora watched him as the little fellow soared upwards.

"Come on, everyone!" the princess called. She ran to get a better view of the watch tower, with Phillip and the others following closely behind.

Everyone tried to see Crackle at the top of the tower, but the storm was too dark and strong. Suddenly, they saw huge flames, and they were coming from little Crackle! Gold and red light flashed up into the sky above the watch tower.

Again and again, Crackle blew his flames until, at last, Phillip shouted. "I see King Stefan and the Queen! They're almost here!"

Everyone hurried to greet the visiting royals.

"The tower light saved us!" King Stefan exclaimed. "I need one like it!"

At that moment Crackle flew happily to join in the fun.

"Well, there he is! Our new tower light," King Hubert said with a laugh.

"A dragon?" King Stefan asked. "But dragons are danger –"

"Not Crackle," Aurora interrupted. "He's a brave and helpful dragon!"

That night at the ball, Crackle lit the candles, warmed food and kept the fireplace blazing. King Hubert and the fairies were so pleased that they took turns scratching Crackle beneath his chin.

As Prince Phillip and Aurora danced, Crackle trotted beside them. Outside, it was cold and stormy. But inside, everyone was happy and warm – especially Crackle the helpful dragon.

The End

Ariel's Dolphin Adventure

By Lyra Spenser
Illustrated by IBOIX and Andrea Cagol

"Oh, Eric! This is wonderful!" Ariel said excitedly as she twirled around the ballroom with her prince. "I can dance with you and see the ocean!"

"Do you miss your sea friends?" he asked.

"Sometimes," Ariel replied a bit sadly. "But I love being with you."

Bright and early the next morning, Prince Eric found Ariel walking along the beach. He knew that she was hoping to see Flounder and Sebastian, as well as her other friends. Sadly, they were nowhere in sight.

Eric caught up with his princess and hugged her as he watched the white-capped waves crashing hard against the shoreline.

"It's rough out there today. If I were a fish, I think I might be too scared to come close to shore," Eric said gently. "Don't worry, Ariel. We'll figure out a way to bring together land and sea. You deserve the best of both worlds."

Later that day, Eric and Ariel went
for a walk.

"I was thinking about what you
said earlier," Ariel said. "I want to show you
something." She led him straight to a quiet,
beautiful little lagoon.

Eric grinned. "I almost kissed you for the first
time here."

"Eric, do you think my friends would feel safer
visiting me here?"

Eric rubbed his chin. "Hmmm. Maybe."

A few weeks later, Eric found Ariel walking along the beach again.
"Come with me," he said. "I have a surprise for you."

He took her right to the lagoon. It now had a big wall to keep out dangerous sea creatures like sharks, but it also had a gate so that Ariel's friends could enter the lagoon. In fact, Flounder, Scuttle and Sebastian were there to greet her!

"Oh, Eric!" Ariel gasped. "I love it!"

Ariel was so excited that she waded into the water.

Then she stopped, seeing something else in the lagoon. "Look!" she exclaimed. As they watched, a baby dolphin leaped out of the water! "He's just a baby. I wonder where his mother is."

Flounder swam across the lagoon, but the baby dolphin raced away.

"Poor little guy," Flounder said. "He seems scared of me."

"We should find his mother right away!" Ariel said as she gently coaxed the baby to swim over to her.

"I bet she's on the other side of that wall. Don't worry, Ariel!" Flounder said. "We'll find her!"

But Sebastian and Flounder couldn't find the dolphin's mother. "Oh, Ariel! This is terrible," Sebastian said a few days later. "We have looked everywhere under the sea, but cannot find the baby's mother. King Triton will be so angry!"

Ariel was watching the little dolphin swim slowly around the lagoon. Heartbroken, she knew that the confused baby was looking for his mother.

Later that night Ariel awoke to the sound of a loud clap of thunder. From the safety of the palace, she saw terrible, high waves crashing to the shore.

"Ariel?" Eric asked. "Are you worried about that baby dolphin?"

"Oh, Eric, I am. He must be terrified," she shuddered in reply. "We need to go to him. And, Eric? I need to ask my father for help."

Eric felt terrible. He now understood that he had made a bad decision by closing in the lagoon. He followed Ariel into the stormy night, ready to help in any way he could.

When they arrived at the lagoon, Flounder was trying to calm the frightened baby dolphin.

"Go to the baby dolphin, Eric," Ariel said gently. "He feels safe with you." Ariel looked into her prince's eyes, letting him know that she trusted him with her sea friends.

Ariel climbed carefully out onto the wall of the lagoon and called to all the sea creatures. "Help me, please!" she cried out. "I am Ariel, princess of the seas. I need my father, King Triton. Please help!"

Below the surface, sea creatures raced to find King Triton.

Eric tried to keep the baby dolphin safe from the crashing waves. Holding him, Eric led him to the calmer waters near some rocks.

Suddenly there was a flash of light, and the storm calmed.

King Triton had arrived at the lagoon.

"What has happened here?" King Triton roared.

Eric looked down humbly. "It is entirely my fault, Sir," he explained. "I built this wall to make a nice place for Ariel to visit her friends. I was wrong."

The king of the seas glared at Eric. Then with a hint of a smile, he added, "Well, you are human, after all."

With a wave of his trident, King Triton called to all the dolphins and they quickly found the baby dolphin's mother! Frantically, she tried to get into the lagoon.

"Oh, dear!" Ariel exclaimed. "The gate won't open! She can't get in!"

Eric looked at King Triton. "Do you mind?"

"Not at all," the king replied. "Swim back, everyone!" He raised his trident and blasted down the wall.

There was no royal ball that night at the palace. Instead, Eric and Ariel returned to the lagoon and danced under the sparkling stars.

"I love this place," Ariel said to her husband. "Thank you."

Just then the baby dolphin and his mother entered the lagoon, surfaced, and playfully splashed the prince and princess.

"I think that means we are forgiven!" Ariel laughed.

The End

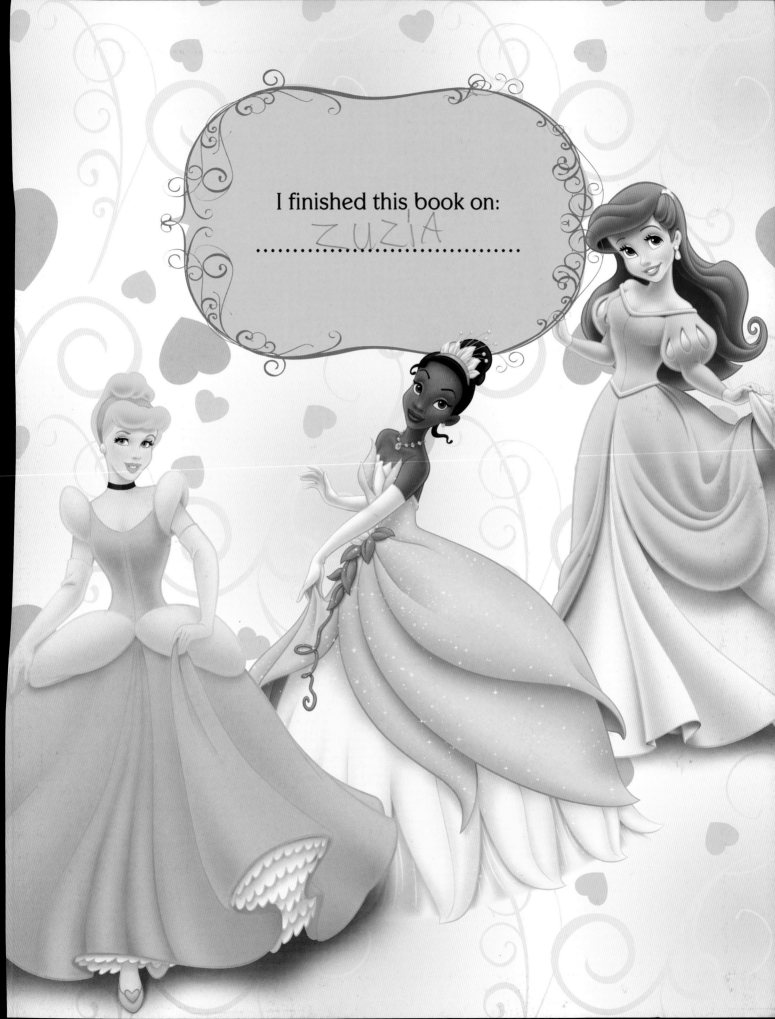

I finished this book on:

ZUZIA

....